A challenge

"You're gross, Harry Spooger!" Mary groaned. "And you're not a very good detective either. Remember the case of the groom? You told us our teacher was marrying Mr. Marks."

"He did get the first name right," Song Lee said. "Mark."

"Well, he got the last name wrong," Mary complained.

"So you think solving a mystery is easy?" Harry asked.

"Not easy," Mary said, "but doable. At least I wouldn't botch up the most important thing."

"Okay, Mare, I have a challenge for you. I'll give you a mystery to solve, and we'll see how well *you* do."

OTHER BOOKS IN THE
HORRIBLE HARRY SERIES

HORRIBLE HARRY
and the Secret Treasure

BY **SUZY KLINE**
PICTURES BY **AMY WUMMER**

PUFFIN BOOKS
An Imprint of Penguin Group (USA) Inc.

PUFFIN BOOKS
Published by the Penguin Group
Penguin Young Readers Group, 345 Hudson Street, New York, New York 10014, U.S.A.
Penguin Group (Canada), 90 Eglinton Avenue East, Suite 700,
Toronto, Ontario, Canada M4P 2Y3 (a division of Pearson Penguin Canada Inc.)
Penguin Books Ltd, 80 Strand, London WC2R 0RL, England
Penguin Ireland, 25 St Stephen's Green, Dublin 2, Ireland (a division of Penguin Books Ltd)
Penguin Group (Australia), 250 Camberwell Road, Camberwell, Victoria 3124, Australia
(a division of Pearson Australia Group Pty Ltd)
Penguin Books India Pvt Ltd, 11 Community Centre,
Panchsheel Park, New Delhi - 110 017, India
Penguin Group (NZ), 67 Apollo Drive, Rosedale, Auckland 0632, New Zealand
(a division of Pearson New Zealand Ltd.)
Penguin Books (South Africa) (Pty) Ltd, 24 Sturdee Avenue,
Rosebank, Johannesburg 2196, South Africa

Registered Offices: Penguin Books Ltd, 80 Strand, London WC2R 0RL, England

First published in the United States of America by Viking,
a division of Penguin Young Readers Group, 2011
Published by Puffin Books, a division of Penguin Young Readers Group, 2012

1 3 5 7 9 10 8 6 4 2

Text copyright © Suzy Kline, 2011
Illustrations copyright © Viking Children's Books, 2011
Illustrations by Amy Wummer
All rights reserved

THE LIBRARY OF CONGRESS HAS CATALOGED THE VIKING EDITION AS FOLLOWS:
Kline, Suzy.
Horrible Harry and the secret treasure / by Suzy Kline ;
pictures by Amy Wummer.
p. cm.
Summary: Third-grader Harry thinks of a way to patch up a conflict with his schoolmate
Mary and include his friends in a fun detective case with rewards for everyone, including
Grandpa.
ISBN: 978-0-670-01181-0 (hc)
[1. Mystery and detective stories. 2. Friendship—Fiction. 3. Schools—Fiction.
4. Grandparents—Fiction.]
I. Wummer, Amy, ill. II. Title.
PZ7.K6797 Hnsh 2011
[Fic] dc—22 2010021256

Puffin Books ISBN 978-0-14-242021-8

Set in New Century Schoolbook
Printed in the United States of America

For my beautiful granddaughter,
Saylor Elizabeth Hurtuk,
who loves to write letters.
You are a treasure!
I love you!
Gamma

Special appreciation to . . .

Sean Quinn, music teacher at Shelter Rock Elementary School in Manhasset, New York; my dear husband, Rufus; my wonderful editor, Catherine Frank; and her hardworking assistant, Leila Sales.

Contents

It All Started at the School Store

Whenever there is a mystery in Room 3B, my friend Harry tries to crack the case. He thinks he's a detective like Sherlock Holmes or Sergeant Friday on old-time TV.

But this mystery, the one I'm going to tell you about, Harry didn't even try to solve.

He didn't have to.

Harry *was* the mystery!

It all started on a Monday morning in February. It was Room 3B's turn to go to the school store. A small group of us who had money lined up at the door of our classroom. Naturally, Harry was first in line.

"I know exactly what I want," he said, holding a fistful of quarters.

"Me too," Mary said, standing behind him. She had a pink beaded coin purse.

"I'm getting a monster eraser," Sid added, holding a nickel and three pennies. I didn't think he had enough money, though.

As we walked down the hall, I checked my pocket. "I have thirty-five cents to spend," I said. "I think I'm getting the red rocket pen."

"Cool, Doug," Harry replied. Then he flashed a toothy smile at the volunteer mom and two fifth graders who sat at the table in the hallway. One of the kids was in charge of the cash box. Two tall shelves of school stuff were set up behind them. "I'd like one of the Magneto Pals," Harry said, pointing to the top shelf of three-inch animals. "The cat, please."

"It's your lucky day," the fifth-grade girl said. "It's our last cat with magnetic paws."

Harry grinned as he handed her four quarters.

Mary's eyeballs bulged. "Oh no! That's the only one I need to complete my set of six."

We all looked at the animals hugging the straps of Mary's backpack. She had paired each of their magnetic paws together. The monkey, lion, frog, dog, and pig held on tightly as Mary moved from place to place. Harry shrugged. "Well, I've been working hard for it, Mare. I washed Grandma Spooger's pots and pans for a week. I don't care about having a set of Magneto Pals. I just want the one that looks like my cat."

Harry was right. It did look like the Goog. It was gray with black stripes.

Song Lee looked into Mary's sad eyes. "Maybe you could order another one," she suggested.

Mary looked hopeful. "May I?" she asked the volunteer mom.

"I'm so sorry, dear," she answered. "The cat is being discontinued."

Everyone felt bad for Mary, but thanks to Harry, I got my red rocket pen, and Sid got his purple monster-head eraser. Harry loaned me fifteen cents, and Sid a dime. Song Lee and ZuZu got pocket notebooks for fifty cents each.

"I'm saving up for the orange troll eraser next," Sid announced.

Song Lee was eyeing the ladybug eraser.

"Well, thanks for your business, guys," the fifth-grade boy said.

"You didn't get mine," Mary grumbled, holding her dollar bill in her fist.

As we walked back to Room 3B, Mary glared at the back of Harry's head.

Pepperoni Eyeballs

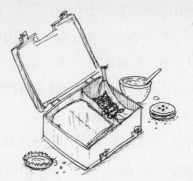

Things got worse at noontime when we were all eating in the cafeteria.

I could almost see the steam coming out of Mary's ears as Harry opened his lunchbox. He had his Magneto Cat attached inside it. Harry had even given him a name. "All right, Googie!" he exclaimed. "Grandma packed me a pepperoni sandwich. Want a bite?" Harry held his sandwich up to his Magneto

Cat's mouth and made eating noises. "Mmmmmmm, good!"

Mary frowned as she shoveled a spoonful of cottage cheese into her mouth. Her eyes never left Harry's gray-and-black-striped cat.

No one said a thing until an announcement came over the loudspeaker in the cafeteria.

"Boys and girls, this is your music teacher, Mr. Marks, with a reminder. Please turn in your permission slips if you're planning to join the school orchestra. Practice begins next Monday. Thank you."

I welcomed the news. "Hey, Harry are you going to join the orchestra?" I asked.

"It depends, Doug," he said.

"Depends on what?" I asked.

"How I see things," he replied. Then Harry took two slices of pepperoni out of his sandwich and placed them over his eyeballs.

"You can't see anything now," Mary groaned.

"Oh yes I can," Harry said. "My inner thoughts. A detective like me has to view things differently. Why do you think they call us private eyes? That's what we use, a third, private eye for making good decisions."

"Puhleese!" Mary snapped. "'Private eye' is just another name for detective."

"Well," ZuZu said, "Harry does have a point."

"I think having a third eye would be cool," Sid said. "I wish I could be a detective."

After a long pause, Harry added, "I might join the orchestra."

"All right!" I cheered.

Mary made a face. "I bet you've never played an instrument."

Harry didn't say a word. He just took the pepperoni slices off his eyeballs and popped them in his mouth. There was some mayonnaise left on his eyelids.

Song Lee giggled as soon as she noticed it.

"You're gross, Harry Spooger!" Mary groaned. "And you're not a very good detective either. Remember the case of the groom? You told us our teacher was marrying Mr. Marks."

"He did get the first name right," Song Lee said. "Mark."

"Well, he got the last name wrong," Mary complained.

"So you think solving a mystery is easy?" Harry asked.

"Not easy," Mary said, "but doable. At least I wouldn't botch up the most important thing."

"Okay, Mare, I have a challenge for you. I'll give you a mystery to solve, and we'll see how well *you* do."

Mary rolled her eyes. "I have no interest in being a detective, Harry."

"But I'll make it an exciting case with a *secret treasure*."

Harry noticed the word *treasure* got my attention.

"And you could have as many assistants as you want . . . *even* Doug, who has helped me with all my cases."

Mary bit into a long stalk of celery. She didn't seem too interested.

"I'll even give you a couple of clues," Harry added. "Pink ones."

When Mary continued crunching, Harry raised one finger. "Of course," he said, "there will be a reward if you *do* solve the case."

"Reward?" Mary laughed. "What reward could you possibly come up with that would interest me? A dead earwig? I don't think so!"

Harry began petting Googie. "Oh, I think I could come up with something."

Mary's jaw dropped. "Your *Magneto Cat* would be the reward?" she gasped.

"It would," Harry replied.

Mary was so excited she meowed.

"Wait a minute," she said, pointing the long stalk of celery at Harry. "What's in it for you if I don't solve it?"

"You stop bringing up the groom case I didn't crack, *and* you make me a poster that says, 'Harry Spooger Is the Third-Best Detective in the World.'"

Mary rolled her eyes. "Well that won't happen, because I'm going to solve your mystery. But I am curious: Who are the first-and-second best detectives?"

"Sherlock Holmes is the best, and Sergeant Friday from old-time TV is the second-best detective."

"What about Miss Marple?" Mary snapped. "She's the best detective that Agatha Christie wrote about. I know because my grandmother has all her books and all the Miss Marple DVDs."

"Agatha Christie also wrote about Hercule Poirot!" Sid added. "My stepdad told me so. Hercule Poirot is a French-speaking detective who has a curly mustache and a derby hat. My stepdad always watches his movies. You know my last name, LaFleur, is French. My stepdad has taught me all kinds of French words!"

"Okay, Mare and Sid," Harry replied. "The poster should say I'm the *fifth*-best detective in the world."

"It's a deal," Mary said.

"It's a deal," Harry repeated. And they shook hands.

"I'll bring pink clues about the secret treasure tomorrow morning. Meet me at the bottom of the playground ramp."

"I can't wait," Mary replied. And then she looked at the rest of us. "I am offering a reward to anyone who's willing to help me with my first case: A fifteen-

cent eraser of your choice at the school store."

"Cool!" Sid said. "I can get my orange troll eraser."

"That's so nice to give us each a prize," Song Lee said. I knew she wanted that ladybug.

Ida, ZuZu, Dexter, and I all put two thumbs up for "The Case of the Secret Treasure." We welcomed the adventure!

Harry just petted Googie's head and smiled.

The Secret Treasure
in the Suitcase

The next morning was Tuesday. We waited for Harry out on the playground.

ZuZu and Song Lee had their new notebooks in hand.

Sid was taping a black mustache under his nostrils. It curled up a little on the ends. "I got this from a party store."

"Is it really necessary?" Mary asked.

"Hercule Poirot wears one."

"Okay," Mary said, taking a deep

breath. "I'm glad you're all up for 'The Case of the Secret Treasure.'"

"*Oui! Oui!*" Sid exclaimed.

"Here comes Grandma Spooger's truck," I said. It made a lot of noise.

We watched Harry hop out and reach for something in the back of the truck.

A big brown suitcase.

Harry carried it quickly down the ramp. His Magneto Cat was attached to its handle.

Mary noticed the cat right away. "Googie will soon be mine," she said, rubbing her hands together.

When Harry saw us, he flashed a toothy smile. "Hey, guys. Nice mustache, Sid. Well, here's your case!" And he carefully set the brown suitcase down in front of us.

"Huh?" we all replied.

"There is a secret treasure inside that is very important to me. All you have to do is figure out what it is."

Sid immediately tried to open it up, but the suitcase was locked.

Harry grinned. "You would need this," he said, pulling a key out of his pocket. It had pink nail polish dabbed on it. "But I'm afraid it's for my use only."

"Well, this case is impossible!" Mary objected.

"Not impossible," Harry said. "You

just need to use your private eye, Mare. Perhaps this key could be your first clue?"

"Huh?" Mary replied.

"That key is our first clue. It's got pink on it!" Sid exclaimed. "And speaking of colors, Hercule Poirot says it's important to use your little gray cells. I just used mine."

"That's what our brain is made up of," ZuZu said. "Gray matter."

Mary blew up her bangs.

I looked down at the piece of paper taped onto the front of the suitcase. The writing on it said:

Go see pink llc

"That must be our second clue," I said.

Harry grinned. "Man, it's the best

clue I could give you guys. I spelled the secret treasure out for you!"

"I'm writing those twelve letters down," ZuZu replied.

"Me too," Song Lee said.

I shook my head. What secret treasure could those twelve letters possibly spell?

"Will you answer questions?" Mary quizzed.

"Maybe," Harry said.

"Can we pick the suitcase up?" Ida asked.

"Sure, just be careful," Harry cautioned.

Ida picked up the suitcase. "It's kind of heavy, but it doesn't rattle."

Harry held up one finger. "Of course not. I have the secret treasure padded in there."

Mary's eyes widened. "I wonder if it's something old."

"Could be, Miss Marple," Harry replied.

Mary smiled. She liked being compared to a famous female detective.

When the school bell rang, we quickly followed Harry and his suitcase up the school steps.

Sid, who was right behind him, spotted the next pink clue first. "Look," he whispered. "There's a pink piece of paper sticking out of Harry's back pocket!"

The Next Pink Clue

As we were walking down the hallway, Mary pulled us all aside. "We'd better let Dexter pick that pink paper out of Harry's pocket," she whispered. "He's good at things like that."

"True," I agreed, remembering how Dexter beat everyone at pick-up sticks. "Will you do it, Dex?"

"Sure! I pick the strings of my guitar all the time."

When we got inside Room 3B and were hanging up our coats, Harry bent down to set his suitcase safely under his winter jacket.

Song Lee covered her eyes. I think she was nervous about Dexter's picking Harry's pocket.

The rest of us watched Dexter tiptoe up behind Harry. With his thumb and index finger, he very slowly pulled the pink note out of Harry's back jeans pocket.

Suddenly, Sid jumped up and down. "You did it!" he exclaimed.

Mary glared at him.

Harry quickly turned around. "What's up, guys?"

Sid covered his mouth. "Eh . . . Mary fixed my mustache."

"All right," Harry said. "Miss Marple has many talents."

Mary smiled as Harry walked happily to his desk.

"Good thinking, Sid," Mary whispered.

I wondered if Harry was pretending not to know about the pickpocketing.

"Now gather round, guys," Mary said. We huddled in the corner and watched Dexter unfold the piece of pink paper.

"It's folded in *fourths*," ZuZu observed. "That fraction could be a clue."

"Like the key," Song Lee added. "Remember? Harry said that was our first pink clue."

Both ZuZu and Song Lee recorded their observations in their notebooks.

As soon as Dexter opened the pink note, we saw what it was.

"A book reserve notice!" Mary complained. "It can't be our next clue."

I was familiar with it. Our librarian, Mrs. Michaelsen, sent us a pink note when a book we requested came back to the library. A purple notice meant a book was overdue.

Harry suddenly reappeared. "Excuse me," he said. "I believe that's mine." And he snatched the pink paper back.

Everyone clammed up, except for Mary. "The note was pink. We're checking all leads. We have to go where our investigation takes us. We were going to return it to you."

Harry flashed a toothy smile. "Glad to see you guys found my next clue. Hope it was helpful."

As soon as Harry left, ZuZu lowered his voice. "Did anyone see the title?"

We all shook our heads.

"I can't believe I didn't read it!" Mary groaned.

Harry was right. It wasn't easy being a detective!

Song Lee's Detective Work

While Miss Mackle was taking atten-
dance and getting the lunch count, Song
Lee was working hard at her desk. I
leaned over the aisle to check what she
was writing in her notebook.

Go see pink llc

pill Geek cons

slick pen loGe

ok pencils leG

Go spleen Kilc

Go spill Keen c

sinG cell poke

"What are you doing, Song Lee?" I asked.

Song Lee looked up from her writing. "I'm trying to solve Harry's case. The answer might be here somewhere. Maybe Harry just scrambled up the twelve letters."

I nodded my head. "Stick with it," I said. "It's the only lead we have right now."

And then as I leaned back and looked

at the day's agenda on the blackboard, I noticed something.

Hmmm, I thought. Maybe we could still find out what that special book was that Harry had on reserve.

First thing that morning, Miss Mackle read us some fables and then called us over to the moon rug in the corner. It was Ida's turn to be the VIP, which meant she got to sit in the director's chair and be the teacher's helper all day. Sid hurried over. He wasn't wearing his mustache anymore. He had it in his shirt pocket though. I could see some black hairs sticking out. I sat on the rug next to Song Lee. I was curious if she was making any progress with that coded message. She had her  notebook with her, and showed me the latest combination of letters she had come up with:

KinG sleepo lc

Harry was sitting next to me on the other side. He had his eyes closed and acted like he was in a deep sleep.

Song Lee and I giggled.

"Boys and girls," Miss Mackle said.

"The past week, we've been reading Aesop's fables. Did you like the one about 'The Crow and the Pitcher'?"

Ida clapped her hands. We all looked up at her like she was queen for a day. "I loved it!"

"Did you? Why?" the teacher asked.

"The crow was clever," Ida replied. "He kept dropping pebbles in the pitcher to make the water level higher."

Song Lee closed her notebook. "I was happy the crow kept trying," she said softly.

"That el tweeto finally got a drink!" Sid exclaimed.

Harry made a face. He was probably thinking of all the times Sid called him a canary, or el tweeto.

Mary told the moral. "Little by little

you can solve problems." Then she looked at us. "Just like a good detective keeps working at a case."

We all nodded. We weren't giving up.

"It's ten o'clock," Ida chimed in. "Time to go to the library."

"Thank you," Miss Mackle said. "Please line up the class, Ida."

"Okay, if you have . . . a note from the librarian, you may line up." Harry was the first one to the door, carrying his pink library slip. "If . . . your birthday is in the fall, you may line up."

I leaned over and whispered to Mary and ZuZu, "This is our chance to get another look at that book Harry has on reserve. It could be our biggest clue!"

Keying in on the Note

As we entered the library, Mrs. Michaelsen had half a dozen books on display about fables. "A little bird told me Miss Mackle's class was reading Aesop," she said, greeting us.

"Was it a crow who told you?" Harry asked.

Mrs. Michaelsen laughed. "Yes, it was. And it was a thirsty one."

Harry grinned as he stepped up

to the librarian's circular desk. We stayed right behind him. "I've come for the book I had on reserve," he said, handing the librarian his pink notice.

"Good," Mrs. Michaelsen said. "It just came in yesterday."

Harry blocked our view as the librarian checked the book out for him. "Hope you enjoy it," she sang.

"Thank you!" Harry sang back.

Mary scowled. "I hate it when people are in a good mood and I'm not."

Dexter shook his head. "We didn't even get a chance to see the title, and Harry has the book hidden under his arm now."

Suddenly, Mary made an observation. "Wait a minute. Why were they were singing? Could that be a clue?"

Mary snapped her fingers. "Of course it is! The singing goes with Harry's other clues, the word *key* and the note being folded in fourths. Fourths are quarters. The clue is quarter notes! Harry's book must be about *music*!"

Song Lee and Ida clapped their hands.

"Cool!" Dexter said. "I wonder if he wants to read about Elvis Presley and guitars."

I lowered my eyebrows. "That's a first," I said. "I've never seen Harry check out a music book before. Vultures, yes. Tasmanian Devils, yes. Earwigs, yes. Music? Never."

"Well, he did!" Sid said. His mustache was back on his upper lip. "I just peeked over Mrs. Michaelsen's shoulder and saw the title on her computer."

"What was it?" we all demanded.

"*The Kids' Easy Songbook*."

"Bingo!" I said.

"Good work, Sid!" Mary exclaimed. "Now we know for sure that Harry's secret treasure has something to do with music."

"You mean *très bien*," Sid said, curling his mustache. "That means 'very good' in French."

"Yes, *très bien*, Sid," Mary repeated. She was in a much better mood. "Okay," she continued, "let's see if we can find out more information about Harry's suitcase. We should be asking you a few questions, Doug. You're Harry's best friend."

"Harry has more than one best friend," I replied, looking at Song Lee. She knew a lot about him too.

"Have you ever seen Harry take that brown suitcase anywhere before?" ZuZu asked.

I sank down in the closest chair and thought about it. I needed time to use my gray cells.

Finally, I spoke up. "Actually, I have. Sometimes when I meet Harry in the morning, I look into Grandma Spooger's truck as they drive up."

"What do you see?" Mary inquired.

"The brown suitcase."

"Every time?" ZuZu asked.

"No . . . maybe once a week."

"On . . . Wednesdays?" Song Lee suggested.

"Yes!"

Mary squeezed next to me in my library chair. Her nose was practically

touching mine. "What happens on Wednesdays?"

Song Lee and I both knew.

"Harry visits Grampa Spooger!" we said.

Big Plans

Mary clapped her hands. "Of course! Harry visits Grampa Spooger every Wednesday at Shady Pines, and when he does, he brings the suitcase with him."

"Now I know what's inside!" Sid bragged.

"What?" we all replied.

"Harry's long underwear for a sleep-over."

"Nooooo," we moaned.

"You can't have a sleepover at a nursing home," Mary said.

"*C'est dommage*," Sid groaned. "That means 'too bad' in French."

No one remembered that French phrase, but we remembered our visit to Shady Pines.

"We visited Grampa Spooger's nursing home two months ago with our class," ZuZu said.

"Yeah, we sang songs," Dexter replied.

"And did activities about the winter holidays," Ida added.

"We sure did," Mary said. "My mom showed everyone how to play the dreidel game. And now it's time to make plans. Raise your hand if you live within walking distance of Shady Pines. It's just up the hill from our school."

Sid and I raised our hands. Mary did. Song Lee and Ida did, and Dexter did.

"Tomorrow's Wednesday. Let's meet there after school, but," Mary lowered her voice, "don't tell Harry. We want our surveillance to be a secret one. We'll wait for him at Shady Pines, and then follow him inside."

"Can I bring my guitar?" Dexter asked. "I could play a few tunes for Grampa Spooger."

"That's a terrific idea!" Mary said. "We can tell the desk clerk that we want to play an instrument for him."

"*Eggsaylant*," Sid said in his best French accent.

"*Instrument*." Song Lee repeated the word softly. Then she suddenly got out her notebook and made a beeline for the closest library table. She was reworking that group of letters again.

ZuZu got a long face. "I don't live that close to Shady Pines, but maybe Mom would take me if I ask her."

Mary crossed her fingers. "Hope you can join us for a real stakeout. And when we go inside, we might just be able to ambush Harry, and catch him with the suitcase open!"

"Stakeout! Ambush! Man, our investigation is *magneefeesant*," Sid said, curling his mustache.

I couldn't wait for Wednesday either.

The Stakeout

Wednesday after school, we all met at Shady Pines. ZuZu's mom dropped him off at the nursing home. She waved when she saw us.

"Thanks, Mom," ZuZu called out. "I'll meet you in the lobby." Then he looked at us with big eyes. "Is Harry here yet?"

"No," I said. "I heard Grandma Spooger say she had to get gas for their truck and make an appointment with the mechanic. They always go to Joe's

Gas Station at the other end of town. He has the lowest prices."

"There's time to hide then," ZuZu said.

We all ran for the cedar bushes except for Mary. She hid behind the sign that said SHADY PINES in big letters.

A few minutes later, I heard Grandma Spooger pulling up to the curb. It sounded like her truck needed a new muffler. Harry jumped out with his suitcase. "I'll join you in thirty minutes," she hollered. "I made some fresh cookie dough this morning for your grampa's favorite snack—warm oatmeal cookies. I just have to pop them in the oven for fifteen minutes."

"Will you bring some for me, too?" Harry called back.

"I'm bringing the whole batch, Lamb Chop!" she said, leaning out the window.

Then Grandma Spooger took off.

Harry walked up the path to the nursing home carrying his brown suitcase. Googie was attached to the handle and bobbled along the way. The piece of paper with the twelve letters was still taped onto the front. When Harry got to the rubber mat, the glass doors automatically opened and Harry walked right in.

"Okay, you guys," Mary announced, "on the count of twenty, we go inside."

We huddled together and counted.

"Twenty!" we finally said, and tip-
toed onto the rubber mat and then into
the lobby. Harry's back was to us down
the hall as he waited for the elevator.

"Duck in here," Mary whispered.
We hurried into a room called THE
SECONDHAND GIFT SHOP. It was filled with
used knickknacks and costume jewelry.
Mary held up a ladies' hat with a sash.
"I can't believe it! The sign says all
hats are twenty-five cents. And this

one looks like the kind Miss Marple wears on the cover of Grandma's DVD. I'm buying it."

"Look at this one!" Sid placed another hat on his head. "It's a derby hat like Hercule Poirot's."

"Except it's green," Mary groaned. "It's for St. Patrick's Day."

"It still looks like a derby hat," Sid insisted. "I'm getting it." He reached deeply into his pocket. He only had three pennies. "I think I'm a little short."

"You're twenty-two cents short," ZuZu replied.

"Oh, give me what change you have, Sid," Mary grumbled. "I'll pay for the rest."

"*Merci beaucoup*!" Sid said tipping his hat. The price tag dangled from the brim like an earring.

When I looked over at Song Lee, she was fiddling with those letters again. Mary peeked around the door. "Harry's gone! Let's go!"

Quickly, we stepped back into the lobby and checked in at the desk.

"We're visiting Mr. Spooger on the second floor," Mary announced to the lady sitting there.

"We're singing a song to him with my guitar," Dexter added proudly.

"He'll love that!" the lady said, handing us the sign-in book. Dexter took the pen that was attached by a string and started writing his name.

"And I'd like to buy these two hats, please," Mary said, handing the lady two quarters.

"Thank you." The lady clipped off the price tags and dropped them into a manila folder. "Are you wearing your hats today?"

"Oh yes!" Mary said, pulling hers down over her head. Sid did too.

"Lovely," the desk lady replied. Then she went back to reading her magazine.

I got the pen last, so I saw how everyone signed their names in the visitors' book.

Two were phony, but they were fun.

Our stakeout was officially over. Now it was time for ambushing Harry.

Ambushing Harry

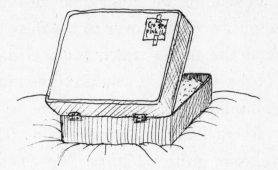

As we walked down the hall, Ida pointed out the hand sanitizer on the little table next to the elevator. We all took some. Sid put a little on his mustache to make it curl up more. It was taped on well this time.

Inside the elevator, I pressed the number 2 for the second floor.

"Now just act normal," Mary said, adjusting her hat. "We're everyday visitors. Got it?"

"Got it!" we replied.

As soon as we stepped out of the elevator, we walked over to the desk and asked the nurse which room Grampa Spooger was in. I couldn't remember the number.

"Room 242," the nurse said. "He'll love your guitar. I know Mr. Spooger loves music. He's in the front row every time we have a concert."

"Cool," I said.

"I love your hats too, and your mustache," she added.

Mary beamed.

Sid said *merci beaucoup* again.

Song Lee quickly finished writing something in her notebook. "I think I just got it!" she squealed.

"*Shhhh!*" Mary said, stopping all of us midway down the hall. "We want

to ambush Harry, and catch him with his suitcase open. No more talking. We don't want Harry to recognize our voices. We want him to think we're just someone from the nursing staff stopping by."

All of us pantomimed zipping our lips.

When we got to Room 242, Mary pointed to Ida and motioned for her to knock.

Ida knocked three times.

When no one answered, Mary pointed to me.

I banged my knuckles on the door. I knew Grampa Spooger was hard of hearing and wore a hearing aid. Lots of times he turned it off because it buzzed.

"Maybe they're not in there," ZuZu whispered ever so softly.

"Let's find out," Sid replied, and he turned the doorknob. *"Bonjour?"* he called.

We all walked in hoping to see Harry, but he wasn't there. His suitcase was though, and it was half opened. Grampa Spooger was sitting in a big easy chair by the picture window. We could see the bird cage outside.

"H-h-helloo!" he said. Since he had his stroke, he stuttered.

"Hi, Grampa Spooger," I said, talking into his ear. I could see he didn't have a left thumb. Harry had told us about his war injury.

"Hi, D-d-doug. H-harry's in the

j-john." Grampa Spooger's roommate wasn't there either.

When we heard the toilet flush, we nodded.

Sidney went right over to the suitcase and raised its top all the way up.

Each one of us gasped when we saw what was inside!

The Secret Treasure!

As we stood there staring inside the suitcase, we saw another small case!

It was the shape of a rectangle. A towel was tucked around it. So that's why it didn't move!

"Well hail, hail, the gang's all here!" Harry exclaimed as he exited the bathroom. "Nice hats, Sid and Mare. You guys are really putting two and two together. You figured out where I take my suitcase. Good job! So do you know what the secret treasure is inside?"

"Yes," Mary said. "Music."

"You're close, but that could mean a lot of things," Harry replied. Then he took out the smaller case and set it on his lap. "GRAMPA," he shouted. "I'M GOING TO SHARE YOUR TREASURE WITH MY FRIENDS."

Grampa Spooger smiled and nodded.

Harry continued, "This belonged to my great-grandpa, Sam Spooger, who was a war hero. That's him right over there. I just call him Grampa. He used it during World War II. I always pack it in a larger case to save his old case from getting banged up. Does anyone know what's inside?"

"An instrument," Song Lee said softly.

Everyone looked at her. So that's what she wanted to tell us in the hallway!

"Tell me more!" Harry said.

Song Lee continued. "Well, Dexter gave me the idea in the library. He mentioned the word instrument first. You gave us all the letters to spell it, Harry. You just scrambled them up. It was a matter of using my third eye." Then she and Harry exchanged a smile.

"When I figured out the first letter," Song Lee continued, "it was easier to get the rest of the word right. There aren't too many instruments that start with G."

"G? It's not guitar!" Dexter replied. "I know how to spell that."

"How did you know it started with G?" Mary demanded.

"It was the only letter that was a capital," Song Lee replied. Then she passed her notebook to Harry so he could see her answer.

"The case is cracked!" Harry declared. "Song Lee got it!"

When Mary plopped down on the bed, her hat fell off. "I can't believe I didn't think harder about that one capital letter! You even told us you spelled out the answer, Harry. I just didn't see it!" Mary exhaled a deep breath.

"What instrument is it, then?" she asked.

"I'll show you." Harry unsnapped his grampa's musical case.

"A *xylophone!*" we exclaimed.

"Xylophone doesn't start with a 'G'!" Harry replied. "Tell everyone what treasure the twelve letters spell, Song Lee."

She held up her notebook and showed us the "G" word.

Glockenspiel

"Glockenspiel?" we said.

"Yes. A xylophone has wooden bars. A glockenspiel has metal ones," Harry explained. "Grampa Spooger is teaching me how to read music."

"That's so cool, Harry, but why did you keep it a secret?" I asked.

"I didn't want anyone to know until I could play something. The first few months, I just listened and watched Grampa Spooger play the song 'I'll Be Seeing You.' He knows a lot of neat World War II songs. But now that I can read music, I can play a tune or two myself. So Dex, I see you brought your guitar. Want to do a duet?"

"Sure, Harry. What tune?"

"How about something real easy, like 'Twinkle Twinkle Little Star'?"

"Let's do it!" Dexter said.

Harry opened up his library book to the first page that had the notes to the song.

"Twinkle, Twinkle, Little Star"

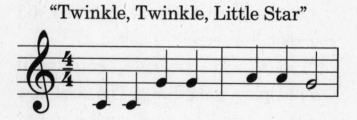

As Dexter strummed his guitar with a pick and Harry plunked his glocken-spiel with a mallet, we all sang along.

Grampa Spooger clapped his hands to the beat. Now I knew why he turned off his hearing aid. Harry played his glockenspiel *very* loudly.

Everyone sang along except for Mary, who was still sitting on the bed looking disappointed. Song Lee was next to her patting her hand.

Harry finally went over to her. "Hey, Mare," he said. "Sometimes a good detective *doesn't* get everything right. I still think you make a good Miss Marple. You just need to wear that hat."

When Mary stood up, Song Lee placed the hat on her head like it was a crown. "You were the leader of our investigation, Mary," she said.

"You thought of things for each one of us to do," Ida added. "You thought of the stakeout and the ambush. And you're giving us erasers for our reward."

Mary and Song Lee and Ida huddled together for a hug.

Harry took Googie off the suitcase handle and walked him over to the girls. "This is yours, Mary!" he said. "Your reward."

Mary took the Magneto Cat and rubbed it against her cheek.

"But . . . I didn't crack the case. Song Lee did."

Song Lee shook her head. "Everyone helped," she said. "It was a team effort. And you were the one who made the discovery of the quarter notes. That got us all thinking about music."

Song Lee and everyone else clapped their hands.

Mary pointed her finger at Sid, Dexter, Ida, ZuZu, Song Lee, and then me. "Song Lee's right. We do make a good team. But, Harry," she added, "I owe you an apology. I'm sorry I bugged you about that groom case. I didn't know how hard it is to get everything right."

"Your saying that means more to me than any poster," Harry said, petting Googie on the head. "Take good care of him."

"I will," Mary said. "But I'm renaming *her* Googette."

Harry flashed a toothy grin. "I thought you would."

"Hey Dex," Harry said. "Can you play, 'Row, Row, Row Your Boat'? It's one of the few tunes I can play by heart on the glockenspiel."

"I sure can! Let's do it on the count of four."

Dexter counted, "A one, and a two, and a three, and a four . . ."

Mary jumped up and waved Googie around like she was the conductor of an orchestra. We all sang while Mary led our mini band, and Harry played his glockenspiel horribly loud.

When we finished our concert, Sid yelled, *"Très bien!"*

I think Grampa Spooger was very smart to turn off his hearing aid.

Epilogue:
The School Orchestra

The following Monday morning all of us detectives showed up for Mr. Marks's school orchestra with our signed permission slips. These were the instruments the music teacher let us play:

Harry Spooger—glockenspiel
Dexter Sanchez—guitar
Song Lee Park—violin
Mary Berg—tuba
Ida Burrell—viola
Sidney LaFleur—French horn
ZuZu Hadad—clarinet

And I got to play the piano!